THE
TIME
TRAVELERS

PHILIP LEVIN

Published by
Doctor's Dreams Publishing
P O Box 4808
Biloxi, MS 39531, USA

Prepared in the United States of America
ICBN: 978-1-942181-23-1
Cover model: Bill Levin, Guru of the Church of Cannabis, Indianapolis, and the cousin of the author.
Cover photo by Neil Smith Photography

THE TIME TRAVELERS

Forward

Thomas Greenwell came to Mississippi in 1832 where he established a large cotton plantation based on slave labor. He died in the Battle of Vicksburg in 1863, leaving the plantation to be run by his two sons. Daniel, the older, has served with the confederacy while Bobby had sided with the North. It quickly became apparent that the two could not agree and a month after their reunion, Bobby mysteriously disappeared.

Daniel had a son, Nathan, who lived a mysterious and reclusive life. When he died in 1975, the mansion remained abandoned until Mallory and Allie Robbins bought it in 2015, refurbishing it, and discovering Bobby

Greenwell's bones buried in a hidden crypt, along with a fortune in Confederate gold. In book one, "The Mysterious Mansion," the Robbins discover the mystery of Bobby's death and put the ghost to rest.

In "The Time Travelers," Mallory and Allie contact Nathan's ghost, who invites them to travel back in time with him to discover information about his mother, of which nothing is known.

Chapter One

2017

"A little off skittle."

Marley stepped back to confirm his wife's impression of his hanging job. The picture, a 19th century rendering of Greenwell, their hometown, listed a bit to the left. He climbed back up on the footstool and realigned it. "Better?"

"Yes."

He looked over at Allie, the warmth of love radiating through his chest. He remembered the day he met her, two years before, within an hour of his arriving in town. She was so shy she could barely look at him. With his first glance, he knew she'd be the one for him.

Looking around the home they'd built, he thanked God for bringing her into his life. Their restored 19th century home, the venerable Greenwell Mansion, seethed with history, from its restored heavy furniture, huge marble fireplace, and immense crystal chandeliers, to the polished woodwork and winding staircase. Their artwork emphasized their shared interest in local history, maps of Alabama, books about the Civil War, and busts of local heroes.

On either side of the fireplace, portraits of the first two Greenwells showed the men in long flock cloaks. Thomas, the founder, stood in front of the house, with the fields of slaves picking cotton on his one side and a champion racehorse he raised on the other. Daniel, his son, was featured on the town green, with the statue the city had built in his honor as background. Nathan, the third and last of the Greenwells, never posed for a portrait, or even a photograph.

Turning back to his wife, he noted that, as usual, she had her nose buried in a book. "What are you reading, Dear?"

She showed him the cover, a paperback called *The Mysterious Mansion*. "It's a ghost story set in an old mansion. Interesting because of our own ghosts." She set the book on the table in front of her and took a sip of the fruit juice there. "I like books where the author describes life in the past. It seems so real, so fetching. Wouldn't it be wonderful to actually go there?"

"Where?"

"Not where. When! You know, the 19th century. Somehow go back to the time when the Greenwells lived here. Wouldn't it be marvelous if we could interview them?"

Marley glanced at the portraits again, and then turned to Allie, his face lit with excitement. "Why don't we try?"

"Try what?"

He came over and sat next to her on the couch, taking both of her hands. "We can't go back in time, but why don't we try to talk with the Greenwells? After all, we know this house is good about communicating with ghosts, right? We had Bobby's and Joseph's ghosts, and also the ring from the grave in the basement. I bet we could somehow communicate with the other Greenwell souls. Their ghosts just might be hanging around here somewhere, right?"

"I don't know," Allie said. "Bobby and Joseph were murdered here and buried behind the fireplace and in the basement. They had reason to haunt the house. Now, we've reinterred all the bodies in the graveyard. Why would their ghosts hang around? It's not as if the others were murdered, right?"

"Oh, I bet they're still around. They all had nefarious deeds – Thomas with all the slaves he maltreated, Daniel murdering his brother, and Nathan – well, who knows what secrets he took to the grave? Let's try and talk with them."

"You mean, like have a séance and call up a Greenwell ghost? Oh, what a marvelous idea!" She grabbed Marley's head in both hands and smacked him strongly on the mouth. "You are an absolute genius, my darling husband! How are we going to go about it?"

"Why don't you see what the Internet suggests?"

Allie opened her laptop and began skimming though various sites. "It says we need personal items of the ones we're trying to contact, and a way for them to talk to us."

Marley snapped his fingers. "Nathan's room! Remember the Ouija Board on the shelf?"

"Of course!" Allie shouted. "There's a crystal and some other stuff on that shelf, too."

"A metal ball, pendulum, bag of tiles, and a doll. I notice details, you know. When do you want to do this?"

"There's a full moon in a week," Allie pointed out. "Let's invite Sidney and Louise over. I bet they'd love to participate in a séance. Having spent his life as a history professor, Sidney'll have all sorts of questions to ask."

"And wherever he goes, Louise follows," Marley noted. "That is, if she can get off duty from the hospital that day. You can cook them a great meal and I'll show off my new wine cellar."

Allie surfed through more Internet pages. "It tells you all about how to set up the room, too. Dim lighting, pentagram, candles, and such. Even if we don't raise a ghost, we'll still have a wonderful dinner party."

"Decided then! I'll give the Ames a call and make sure they have the night free."

"And I'll research the items on Nathan's shelf," Allie said. She placed her laptop on the coffee table and stood, stepping over to kiss Marley again. "You make me so very happy!"

"The feeling's mutual," he said.

Chapter 2

1868

"Boil some water and prepare a stack of clean linen," Louise commanded, as she bustled in, carrying her black bag. "Now where's the patient?"

Daniel gave orders to his house servants to prepare the materials and to lead Louise out to the cabin. As Louise washed her hands in the provided hot water, she studied the pregnant girl's features. The teenager had creamy skin, clearly a mulatto. Lovely dark eyes with long lashes, full luscious lips, and a slightly broad nose, she'd inherited the best of both of her parents' races. Her forehead soaked with sweat, she cried out with each contraction.

Another young girl, eight-years-old, had been assigned to assist. Her eyes wide with fright, she hopped around, cringing every time the pregnant woman moaned.

"What are your names?" Louise asked.

"This be Olive," the young one said. "And I be Jewel. I don't ne'er see a baby born before. Is I gonna get to see it?"

Louise chuckled. "Yes, if you can be brave enough. Can you be brave enough to help me?"

The girl straightened up, puffing out her bottom lip. "Yes ma'am. I be really brave."

"Good. You hold this towel. Don't let it touch the ground, you understand? When the baby comes, you'll hand it to me and I'll wrap the baby in it."

Louise examined Olive, finding her half dilated.

"Is the baby gonna come soon?" Jewel asked, dancing behind them.

"Not yet. Because this is Olive's first baby, it will take a bit longer for her to be able to push out the baby. Would you like to learn how to deliver babies?"

"Yes ma'am. Is you gonna teach me?"

"Maybe when you're a bit older. But for now, pay attention to everything I do."

Louise studied the mother's features carefully. The girl had the Greenwell eyebrows, thick and well sculptured. "How old are you, Olive?"

The girl took a deep breath, recovering from the latest contraction. "I be fifteen, ma'am."

Louise did some quick calculations. It was 1868 now, so the girl was born in 1853. Thomas, known to have sex with his slaves, had been forty-three that year, so likely was this girl's father.

"Do you know who's the baby's father?" Louise asked.

Olive didn't answer, staring at the ceiling. Louise waited patiently, and when the girl began sobbing, she used a clean towel to dry her tears.

"Daniel's cousin, him done visit from Virginia. Master Daniel, he tol' me to make 'im happy." She gave out a few more sobs before looking beseechingly into Louise's eyes. "It hurt! No one tol' me it was gonna hurt!"

Louise checked her charge again, finding the girl had made good progress in her dilation. Sitting back on the provided stool, she asked, "Does Daniel treat you well? Decent beds, food, toilets?"

Jewel nodded. "We git lots of greens and grits, and pork bellies on Sundays."

Olive shrugged. "He better than Master Thomas. No more whippings."

The baby came out wailing, light skin and gorgeous. "Ten fingers, ten toes," Louise announced, wrapping her in the towel Jewel handed her. "What's her name?"

"Ginger!" Olive announced. "Can ah hold 'er?"

"Just a minute." Louise signaled Jewel to come close and handed her scissors. "Cut the cord right here," she instructed, and Jewel did.

Louise wiped off the baby, wrapped her in a clean towel, and brought her to lay beside her mother. The baby snuggled up and fell asleep.

After delivering the afterbirth and ensuring that the girl didn't need sutures, Louise packed up her materials and went into the big house.

Daniel invited her into the dining room where, once settled, one of the servants brought them biscuits and sweet tea. Louise surveyed the area, the cabinets with all the plates and crystals looked the same as they would a hundred and fifty years later. The most obvious difference was that the wallpaper was fresh, instead of removed and painted as Marley and Allie had done. She glanced into the kitchen, finding all its ancient appliances totally different from Allie's improvements.

"You have a fine baby girl," Louise told him. "Mother and child are both doing well. Olive named her Ginger. From the looks of her, she could pass for a whitey."

Daniel nodded. "Good, good. Perhaps she'll be a good house servant then. I was sort of hoping for a boy, though. Having to support another mouth is easier when it's a farm worker."

After a minute of silence, Louise commented, "Olive told me that you had a cousin visit from Virginia about nine months ago."

Daniel didn't look at her. "Yes, my cousin George Kirkpatrick."

Louise waited for him to continue.

Daniel put down his spoon and grunted. "Okay, so I had her sleep with him. That's Southern hospitality, isn't it? I'm not proud of it, but he expected it. I have to keep up customs. Niggers are niggers and whites are whites. We got to keep them separate."

Louise waited until he looked at her before asking, "Do you?"

Daniel glared at her, and then looked away again. "I'm not my father. I try to treat my niggers well. Feed 'em. Give 'em shelter. Even pay 'em a little."

"And have sex with them?"

Daniel shook his head. "No. That was my father. If and when I ever have sex, it will be with a woman I have true feelings for, not one I'm forcing myself on. One who wants me, and maybe one who will have my child."

"A white woman, of course."

"Yes!"

Louise finished her scone and sat back, enjoying her tea. "I notice you don't get out much, don't have people over."

"I'm busy with the planation. I don't have time for tomfoolery." He called out to his servant. "Ethel. Bring us some whiskey."

In a minute the woman brought a bottle and two glasses. Daniel poured shots into both glasses. He downed his quickly and refilled. Louise took a polite sip.

"I have a present for little Ginger," Louise said. She brought a doll out of her satchel and placed it on the table.

Daniel picked it up, turning it around and looking at it in puzzlement. "Can't say I've ever seen a doll like this before. Stringy hair, gingham dress … sort of ugly, isn't it?"

Louise laughed. "It's called a Raggedy Ann. Keep it fresh for her. And here, I have another present. This one is for your son." She brought out a silver metal ball about ten inches in diameter with little slots along its diameter.

Daniel examined it, weighing it in his hands. "This is very nice, very nice indeed. What makes you think I'm going to have a son some day?"

Louise winked. "Call it woman's intuition. Here, these tiles go with it. Keep them safe."

"Very well." Daniel handed her three gold coins. "This is for your services."

She nodded her head in appreciation. "Very generous – thank you, Mister Greenwell. I best be going home. I have my cats to feed."

They stood, shook hands, and Louise left, a knowing smile on her lips.

Chapter 3

1892

Daniel turned up the wick on the kerosene lamp, its flicker creating ominous shadows across the sickroom's drapes. Using a fresh damp cloth, he wiped the bloody drool off of Ginger's chin and neck, rinsed the cloth in a porcelain bowl, and then used it to wipe the sweat off her forehead and chest. She groaned at his touch and opened her yellowed eyes.

"How are you?" he asked.

With the faintest of motions, she shook her head. Her voice, barely audible, strained over every word. "What did the doctor say?"

Daniel remembered the doctor's shake of his head, the furrowed brow, and tightened lips. He hadn't had to say it. Daniel had already figured out that his mistress wouldn't last the night.

"He said he'd be back in the morning with a new medicine that's coming in from Atlanta. Seems to have helped other victims of the yellow fever. You're going to be fine, just hang in there."

Ginger sighed. "You're lying. I can tell I'm nearing my last breath." Reaching out she grabbed onto Daniel's hand, squeezing it tightly. "You won't forget your promise, now? If you care at all for me or your son, this is my dying wish."

Daniel squeezed back, bent down, and kissed her forehead.

She lay back and Daniel watched her struggled breathing. Opening her eyes again, she asked for fresh water. Pouring the last into the glass, he helped her sit up and sip it down. Once she'd settled back, he grabbed the empty pitcher and the porcelain bowl and stepped quietly out of the room.

Downstairs in the main room the two house servants waited. Mabel had been watching Hany playing with two-year-old Nathan and his favorite toy, a shiny metal ball. The child, with no concept that his mother was upstairs dying, giggled with delight as he and Hany rolled the ball back and forth. When Daniel came down, Mabel took the pitcher and bowl from him and headed towards the kitchen.

"Fresh towels, too," he called after her. He turned his attention back to the floor.

"How's the boy?"

"Juss fine, Master Daniel," Hany answered. "He be growin' up strong, like his pa."

Daniel snorted. "Maybe. I just wish he hadn't gotten his skin color from his mother's side."

Hany stood, picking up the boy and tossing him up and down, eliciting peals of laughter. Catching him, he set him gently on the ground. Nathan crawled over to the pile of strange tiles and began stacking them.

"He shore do love 'em tiles and that ball. Where did y'all get 'em, you say?"

Daniel thought back the twenty-four years to the day Ginger was born. He certainly never would have predicted then that he'd fall in love with her.

"There was this strange couple who claimed they came from the far west, California. Spoke funny, dressed funny, strange ideas. He was old, gray haired, wrinkled – nice enough, but always asking questions. Died after a few years. His wife was a midwife."

Daniel paused as Mabel returned from the kitchen with the fresh water and towels. "Take them up and tend to her," he told her. "I'll be up shortly."

Nathan had made a tower with the thirty tiles, clapping with delight, and then kicking it over, scattering the pieces across the room.

"Dat boy shore got character." Hany said with a laugh as he began gathering up the tiles.

"Louise was her name," Daniel continued. "She gave me the ball and tiles the day Ginger was born. She predicted I'd have a son to give them to."

Hany brought the tiles back to Nathan and, sitting on the floor with him, showed how to make them into little card houses. "How you figure she know dat?"

Daniel shrugged. "She knew a lot of things. She performed midwifery for thirty years delivering a couple of hundred babies I bet. She didn't differentiate between niggers or whites. Taught a couple of other women how to be midwives, too, including Jewel, the one who delivered Nathan. Good woman, that Louise."

Mabel called down from the top of the stairs. "Master Daniel. Master Daniel. You'd best come on up now."

Daniel felt his heart thump hard in his chest as he took the mansion's wide staircase two steps at a time. He hurried to the sick room but stopped at the door. Ginger's jaundiced eyes were open, fixed on the ceiling. Her chest didn't move.

He bowed his head and muttered a short prayer, then turned, shut the door, and headed back down the hallway.

"You be wanta me fetch the doctor, Master Daniel?" Mabel called after him.

He shook his head. "No. Let her rest. Tomorrow I'll take her down to the basement and bury her."

He trudged down the steps, his head held high. Using his handkerchief, he dabbed one of his eyes, the only sign he would show of the grief filling his heart. He stopped on the landing, looking down at his son. Nathan, though only an eighth black, had come out with very dark skin and other features of that part of his heritage, including the kinky hair and broad nose.

"Wha' ya gonna do wid Nathan?" Hany asked.

Having officially adopted the boy, the child was now heir to the Greenwell mansion and plantation. But how could this lad ever truly inherit? The townspeople wouldn't accept a colored running everything. So far, he'd made sure no one besides Mabel and Hany ever laid eyes on the boy, keeping his birth secret and the adoption papers hushed in his lawyer's safe.

Daniel thought about the promise he'd made to Ginger. "I've heard about an exclusive boarding school in London," he told Hany. "It'll take me a couple of weeks to prepare, then I think you, Nathan, and me will board a steamer. Nathan will be happy there among people who won't hate him for his skin color. I'll come back and continue making Greenwell my life's project."

"You shore? You willin' to ne'er see your son again?"

Daniel's mouth narrowed in determination. "I'll visit him there every year. Maybe in another twenty years times will be different – niggers can be respected. Until then, he'll be safer overseas."

Chapter 4

2017

In the middle of the spacious living room, Marley had taped the shape of a pentagram, nine feet across. The room's only light, flickering candles at each of the star's points, created an eerie, other worldly atmosphere. Pingy New Age music and sweet burning incense added to the atmosphere. The surrounding overbearing portraits gave ancestral countenance to the night's planned procedures.

Waiting for the other three to come in from the kitchen, Sidney stood in front of the huge marble fireplace. Easily large enough for a man to lie in, it spoke of the parties and celebrations that had marked the mansion's earliest years. Sidney wondered why those parties had ceased when Daniel took over Greenwell Mansion.

"Sorry to leave you alone for so long … had to help Allie clean up," Marley said, coming down from the kitchen. "Is your vision better since the cataract surgery?"

Dr. Ames cocked his head. "How did you know about that?"

"You have a distinctly uneven shave on the left side of your face, the new lens on the right shimmers in the candlelight, and there's still a hint of bloodshot in the whites."

Lifting his glass in a salute, Dr. Ames said, "You're very observant my friend." Sweeping his hand in indication, "You and Allie have done marvels with this old building. The woodwork gleams as if it were installed yesterday rather than 200 years ago."

"A hundred and eighty, actually." Marley walked over to the mantlepiece, rubbing his hand across its gleaming edge. "This piece of solid marble came from Italy. At more than a hundred and fifty pounds a cubic foot, it's estimated to weigh over a ton."

"Can you imagine how much it must have cost to have this dragged up from New Orleans?"

"Ah yes, the Greenwells were quite wealthy," Marley said. "Thomas was driven to make a profit, exploiting slavery to its maximum potential. He built this mansion to showcase his wealth, hosting great parties with politicians and landowners from across the state as guests." He paused to sip his wine. "Standards were different then. He cheated in business, abused his animals, and dehumanized his slaves, yet was highly honored."

Sidney grunted. "I would love to hear his viewpoints. This séance will be fascinating, although, of course, I don't actually expect to communicate with ghosts."

Allie and Louise came into the room bringing plates of *petits* and fresh wine.

"What are you two talking about?" Allie asked, as she refilled Sidney's wine glass.

"Communicating with the dead," Sidney answered. "I was just saying that as an academic I don't believe in the existence of ghosts."

"Oh, they're real all right," Allie said. "After Daniel killed his brother Bobby and their servant Joseph, those two haunted this place until Marley freed their spirits." She stepped over to kiss him on the cheek. "My hero!"

"Let's have another drink before we settle into this," she suggested. Allie refilled their wine crystals with crimson claret and raised hers in a toast. "To the realm of the supernatural."

They clinked and drank.

"Delicious," Sidney remarked, smacking his lips. "I see you're making use of the new wine cellar."

Marley chuckled. "Yep. Once we got Bobby's remains out of the secret tomb behind the fireplace, it turned out to be the perfect spot for the wine cellar."

Allie leaned forward, conspiratorially. "It took Marley less than a week to deposit a hundred bottles!"

Her husband gave a half smirk. "Plenty of room in there for a couple of hundred more."

"You're actually using Bobby's tomb as a wine cellar?" Louise asked. "That sounds sort of creepy. Is it Bobby's ghost we're going to try to raise tonight?"

"No," Marley said. "We've laid Bobby to rest after his 150 years of turmoil. I have a different spirit in mind. Ever since I saw the ghosts in this house, I've been convinced there must be some way to speak with the dead. Nathan obviously thought so. He collected items used for bringing up spirits and kept those objects on a shelf above his bed."

"What kind of items?" Sidney asked.

"Here, I have them in a box."

He directed the others to sit in three of the four chairs at the table in the middle of the pentagram. Once everyone was settled, he opened the box he had resting on the fourth chair. Reaching inside he brought out a rectangle of wood and a glass ornament.

"This is a Ouija board. See how it's mildly worn? Nathan must have used it a few times, but then gave it up. This model has a copyright mark on it of 1930 and comes from France. That was the same year Nathan came back from Europe to live here … he may have brought it with him."

He pulled out a large crystal from the box. Made up of an explosion of yellowish rods curling around each other in the pattern of an exploding atom, it glistened in the candlelight. "This is shattuckite. Those who study the occult say it's essential for communicating with the deceased." He placed it on the table in front of him.

"Who are we going to try to summon?" Sidney asked. "Thomas? I was just saying how I'd love to get his views on Southern morals."

"No, not Thomas," Marley said.

"Sarah?" Louise offered. "I'd love to discuss her views on her philandering husband. Allie told me that he had his own cabin here on the grounds where he had frequent dalliances with his slaves."

"Someone else," the host insisted.

"We considered Daniel," Allie said. "To me, he's the most interesting character of the lot. He killed his brother and the faithful family servant. Yet, except for that, he was a model citizen. He was so generous to the town they built a statue in his honor. He bankrolled his son to live in luxury in Europe from infancy until Daniel's death, thirty-eight years later."

Marley raised his hands as if in a priestly benediction. "Yes, my friends. Those would all be fascinating subjects. But our targeted ghost for tonight's séance will be the third Greenwell, Daniel's son, Nathan."

"It's no wonder he tried to communicate with ghosts," Allie remarked. "He lived in the house with Bobby and Joseph's ghosts all those years."

"Right," Marley agreed. He pulled out four more objects from the box. He handed Sidney a pendulum, a doll to Louise, a snakeskin bag to Allie, and in front of his spot on the table, he placed a silver ball. Moving the box to the floor, he sat in his chair.

Louise giggled. "This Raggedy Ann doll certainly seems out of place among all these weird pieces, don't you think?"

Allie nodded. "Yet it was on the bedroom shelf with these others, so it must have had special meaning to Nathan. Maybe if we can reach his spirit tonight, we can ask him."

Sidney picked up the metal ball giving it a close inspection. "This is certainly an odd piece. It has a compass on one end and slots around the middle."

"We haven't been able to find out anything about it despite extensive searches on the Internet," Marley said.

He asked Allie to open the bag he'd handed her. From it she extracted a tile and handed it to Marley. "Hold the ball as I insert this tile into a slot," he told Sidney. "Feel that?"

Sidney nodded. "Yes, the ball seemed to hum."

"We have no idea why … or what either the ball or the tiles mean."

Allie took a few more tiles from the bag and held them up. "Look, each of the tiles is brightly colored with a strange symbol."

"Maybe they're just children's toys?" Louise suggested.

"Maybe. But even so, where did they come from? Certainly, no one in the nineteenth century could have manufactured them."

"I see there was a purpose in your distribution," Sidney observed. "The pendulum for me, the historian whose life has been devoted to time."

"Yes," Marley said. "Please start it up."

Louise hugged the Raggedy Ann. "Obvious choice for me, the midwife."

Allie ran a few of the tiles through her fingers. "And for the archeologist, a bit of ancient unreadable runes. An excellent choice, my amazing husband."

He blew her a kiss.

"This is how it works," Marley explained. "We each place one hand on the corner of the Ouija board and the other on your object."

"How will we tell if we've made contact?" Louise asked.

"Theoretically, the Ouija marker will move by itself," he explained. "Now close your eyes and empty your minds."

They waited, the spectral music and the clicking of the pendulum counting off each second the only sounds. After two minutes, Marley spoke.

"Nathan Greenwell, you who spent most of your life within these walls, we call upon your spirit. Make yourself heard."

A scraping sound came from the Ouija board and their eyes snapped open. The planchette crawled across the old surface and settled on the H.

"H?" Allie read. "What does that mean? Home?"

The piece quivered and then crept across the board to land on the E.

"It's clearly a message," Sidney said. "He. Give it a moment, we'll hear more."

The Ouija piece moved jauntily to the L, hung out for a moment, made a sweep of the board and settled again on the L.

A shocked silence settled on the crowd.

"Hell?" Marley said. "Is Nathan saying he's in hell?"

The planchette strolled across the board, circling a bit, as if in a tease, and finally settled on the O.

"Hello!" Louise exclaimed. "Nathan's spirit is here and saying 'Hello!' This is amazing!"

"If you think that's so great, wait until you see what's coming down the stairway at you."

They all turned to the British accented voice. Louise screamed. Standing there, as real as if he'd stepped out of a roaring twenties discothèque, a young man shod from shiny top hat down to silvery slats descended step by glorious step. His skin was deep black, eyes of golden brown, and a thick-lipped gracious smile lit up his handsome face.

He came to a stop on the landing, three steps above the floor. Using his silver tipped walking stick to tip his hat, he grabbed it as it fell, sweeping it across his waist below a magnificently executed bow.

"Nathan Greenwell, esquire, at your service. It's good to see you again, Marley and Allie."

Chapter 5

1899

Nine-year-old Nathan walked beside his father, enjoying the throngs of people in Hyde Park. He rarely had a field day, being a foreigner without family at the prep school. All year he'd been looking forward to his father's annual spring visit.

They stopped to admire the huge statue of Achilles, and Daniel asked Nathan if he knew who Achilles had been.

"Looks like some naked fighter. That fig leaf hardly gives much modesty, what?"

Daniel snorted. "You certainly speak like a Brit, boy. I suppose that's to be expected, maybe even desired." He tussled the boy's hair. "Achilles was half-man and half-god, and the greatest warrior of all time. He died in the Trojan War 3000 years ago."

The boy stared up at the statue, impressed with the oversize muscles, the curly hair, and noble features – very British features. "He was British?"

"No, Greek."

"So why is this statue here?"

Daniel looked in the guidebook he'd bought. "It says the statue commemorates the Duke of Wellington's victory over Napoleon." He placed the book back in his overcoat. "You must study history, my son. A well-rounded education will suit you wherever you lead your life."

"I know where I'd rather be leading my life now." Nathan grabbed his father's hand, beseeching with pleading eyes. "Pater, why can't I come home with you? I hate it here. The boys make fun of me, calling me a half-breed who doesn't even have a mother."

Daniel didn't answer, instead leading the boy out of the gardens through the park's iconic Wellington arched grand entrance. They exited onto a busy street with horse-drawn buggies, backfiring cars, and men pushing handcarts. Around them pedestrians strolled, vendors shouted, and storekeepers beckoned. An organ grinder with a monkey sprayed clunky sounds through the air. Tall plane trees grew out of perfect circles in the brick sidewalks.

Daniel swept his hand in front of the landscape. "Here you have the world! Look around you, my son. Sophisticated men in top hats. Fancy women carrying parasols. London is full of commerce and culture. Why would you ever leave this world to be trapped in an old haunted mansion in Alabama, boy? The building's a prison: dusty, angry, and stifling. I'd leave it in a snap if I could."

"Well why can't you? You're clearly rich enough. Just sell the house and come live with me here."

Daniel shook his head. "I'm chained to that house, sentenced to home imprisonment. It's a penance for what my father and I have done."

He raised his handkerchief to his nose and sneezed. "Damn London air. All this coal dust ruins your lungs."

"Still, I could come home for summer holiday, eh, Pater?"

"No." He grabbed the boy's hand and used it to point at a store window across the street. "Come along, I'll buy you a toy."

Nathan snatched his hand away. "Not until you tell me why I can't come visit."

"You're a stubborn little thing aren't you? Get it from your Grandfather I imagine. Very well. I'll be blunt. You must never be seen in Alabama because of your skin color. Here you're just dark. There you'd be a nigger. You don't know what it's like for people who look dark."

Nathan held up his hand examining its back. "Dark? I am dark, verily. My skin color comes from my mother, of course. Why would this matter?"

"It does. Niggers are little better than animals there. I vowed to your mother I'd keep you from all that."

"My mother? Tell me about her, would you please?"

Daniel stared off, not moving as pedestrians flowed around them. One middle-age matron stopped, having noticed the two. She came up and asked if everything was all right.

Daniel shook himself out of his thoughts and assured the woman all was fine. Taking Nathan's hands, he pulled him across the road and into the toy store. Nathan picked out a hand-winding metal carousel. It contained a music box that played a popular tune as the horses galloped in circles around the center.

"Top drawer!" Nathan exclaimed.

They stopped at a small café at the edge of the park and Daniel bought them both scoops of ice cream, served in a small metal bowl with a biscuit on the side. The boy spooned his slowly, swirling the ice crystals in the bowl until they melted.

"This is truly a treat, Pater. Do you not have vanilla ice cream back home?"

Daniel watched the pedestrians: Indians, Chinese, Whites, and Africans, people from all over. Here no one had to step aside for others simply because of their skin color. And yet, he could tell class distinction, the rich whites walked with their noses in the air, the other races, and even the poor whites, with heads bowed.

"Yes, we have vanilla ice cream. However, you wouldn't be allowed to have any. White ice cream is reserved for white people. You can't imagine what it's like, Nathan."

Daniel crumpled his napkin into a tiny ball, his eyes narrowed in anger. "Segregation goes beyond simple rudeness. It's purposeful cruelty. My father used to starve his slaves. He would whip the men and rape the women."

Nathan choked on his ice cream. "Oh Pater! It can't be that bad now?"

Daniel grimaced. "In some ways, it's worse. Sometimes if there's an uppity nigger, some white woman will claim he winked at her. Then the white folks capture that nigger and hang him in a public spectacle. Sometimes two or three of them at once."

He forced himself to relax his clenched fists. Looking into his son's eyes, he said, "As long as I'm alive, your life will be here."

In the evening Daniel took his son and checked him back into the dorm. Just before leaving, he bent and hugged the boy goodbye.

"I love you, Pater," Nathan whispered in his ear.

Daniel caught his breath. "Your accent is different, but those words …. I just realized besides your mother you're the only person who ever said them to me."

"She loved you. Did she love me? I don't have any recollection of her at all."

Daniel placed his hand on Nathan's shoulder. "Your mother was the sweetest, most loving woman I've ever known. But she's gone now, and we must go on with our lives. I wish for you to make your own future, never having to live in the past. Of all people, I know that most intimately, for it is my fate."

From the dorm window, Nathan watched his father walk away. At fifty-five, the man strode a confident pace, head high, purpose radiating with every movement. Perhaps he was right, Nathan considered. Staying away from Greenwell seemed sensible.

But there was still the mystery of his mother. He wanted to know more about that side of his heritage. Why were the people of his mother's race treated so badly in Alabama? He decided he would devote his life to finding out all he could about Greenwell's Antebellum past, and about his mother.

Chapter 6

2017

Nathan sauntered up to the table and looked over the settings. "Top drawer! I gander you've gathered the essentials: crystal, pendulum, runes, and the Silver Globe. Because the Ouija board is so wurp, I deemed it facile to spot an appearance."

He looked around at the group, who stared back in either horror or fascination, as due their nature.

"What? Cat got your tongues? You called this petting pantry, you know. It's not as if I'm a barger."

He strolled around the room as the four watched. "Top cheese what you've done with the place. Restored to old glory. I imagine the basket's overflowed with electricity and plumbing since my day, what? Had a wicked time installing a loo down here."

He faded through the door into the bathroom and materialized back out again. "Hostsy-totsy for certain."

Marley spoke, "If we let go of the Ouija board, will you fade away?"

Nathan narrowed his brows. "Don't imagine so, dames and gents. Give it a try if it's your noodle."

The four let go and Nathan nodded. "Right ho. You've called me up, might be an icy mitt offing me again."

Sidney stood and stepped over to the ghost, reaching out to touch him. His hand went right through. "Marley, this isn't a fancy hologram display, now is it? I wouldn't put that past you."

"No, no," Nathan said. "I assure you old chap, everything's Jake. And, by-the-by, I know Marley and Allie, but who might you be?"

Sidney, though clearly still skeptical, made introductions. "I'm Sidney Ames and this is my wife, Louise. I'm a retired historian with a special interest in mid-nineteenth century history and Louise is a nurse midwife at the local hospital."

Nathan smiled. "Aha. We haven't met, but I do know a bit about you, Louise. You hobnobbed with the old pater. That would be an interesting tale, though, of course, you're napping."

Marley and Allie stood as well, although Louise continued to sit, clutching the doll. Allie asked, "I don't suppose you'd like something to drink?"

Nathan put his head back and chortled. "Ah, little bearcat, as gracious as ever. No, in this form I don't eat, drink, breathe, or use any other bodily functions. I do miss the gasper and jorum of skee. By-the-by, eye the outfit? Bee's knees, wouldn't you say?"

"Yes, quite darb," Marley said. "Tell us how you know us."

Nathan tossed his hat towards the divan, though instead of landing on it, the hat passed on through, eventually hovering in the air beyond. "Interesting effect, that," he noted.

Turning back to Marley, he said, "Well, that's a bit of a Sweeney. And you know what is said about time travel. If you're in-the-know, you'll tumble in the pit. Best await the ciné."

"Time travel!" Marley and Sidney shouted simultaneously.

"That's not possible," Sidney said. "As you just said, if one could go back in the past, he'd change history, and perhaps cease to exist in the present. It's an irrefutable paradox."

"This you say to a ghost, looking to be thirty-five, dressed in an outfit from the 1920s? Eh? Where's your whoopee, old chap?"

Louise spoke for the first time since the ghost appeared. "You say you've met Marley and Allie in the past, and that I met your ancestors. Does that mean we will be traveling to the past? And in separate trips?"

Nathan gave her a wink. "Now you're on the trolley. Those trips will be sockdollagers, and that's the verified."

Louise asked, "Can't you speak in modern English so we know what you're saying?"

"Ah, as you command, little bluenose."

The ghost changed, aging into a septuagenarian, gray hair, striped pajamas, and terrycloth dressing gown. His posture now affected a shoulder stoop, a saddened expression on his aged-lined face. In one hand he held a smoldering cigar that added its odor to the room. He sighed.

"Better?" His voice now had less of a British accent, deeper and slower, as if stress and aging had affected every part of him.

"Well, more what I would expect a ghost to look like," Louise admitted.

"We called you here," Marley said, "in hopes of getting information about these objects. Are they involved in the time travel?"

Nathan hobbled over to a chair and settled onto it, his form sometimes sinking an inch or two into the cushion, at other times rising and hovering just a bit in the air above. "It's a story that begins in 1922. I had graduated from the Sorbonne, a degree in history, like you, Dr. Ames, and, indeed, specializing in recent American studies. Can you conjecture as to my motivation?"

Marley spoke up. "Coming from the Greenwell family, I would guess you wanted to know about your own heritage, especially your maternal side. Allie and I have made extensive studies of the Greenwells, and your father in particular. He never married your mother, did he?"

Nathan raised an eyebrow. "You're very astute, Marley. I remember that from our adventure together. Yes, that's right. I was two years old when she died, and afterwards my father sent me to live in England. He refused to talk about my mother and kept me from coming home. I decided the only way to find out was to study the supernatural, in other words, learn to communicate with the dead."

He took a moment to rest, his eyes staring off as he envisioned some dark history. The four waited on him, the sounds of the music and the metronome echoing in the hallway. Pointing to the latter, he said, "How about turning that thing off for a bit?"

Sidney complied.

"He was quite rich, dear old Pater, though I never did find out where my father got all his money. There were rumors he had brought back gold from the war. Well, whatever, I had all the resources I needed and decided to seek out all the occult practitioners throughout Europe. Most of them were frauds, of course. Smoke and mirrors. Finally, though, outside a little village in Bavaria, deep in the Black Forest, I found an eclectic old man who started me on the road to discover the secrets you'll soon learn."

All waited in anticipation, but Nathan seemed to have drifted off into his own thoughts again.

"And what was that secret?" Marley finally asked.

Nathan shook his head, as if clearing deep visions. He floated over to the bookshelf and skimmed his finger along the top row. He hovered next to a volume with an ancient decorated spine.

"This book contains instructions on how to use the Silver Globe, runes, and pendulum. Marley and Allie, you two must follow those directions precisely and meet me back in time."

"Where and when are we to go?" Allie asked.

"We're going back to meet my mother, a week before I'm born. Aim for noon, March 12, 1890, on the town green."

"What about the doll?" Louise asked, holding it up.

"Ah, that's another story." A tear rolled down Nathan's ghostly cheek. "Yes, indeed. That's a whole different tale."

And with that, he faded away.

Chapter 7

1930

Leaning against a tree, Nathan drank the last of his water canister. After two hours worming his way through Bavaria's Black Forest, he needed a rest.

"What I bloody well need," he muttered, "is a dab of brandy served next to an overstuffed chair by a comforting fire. Path indeed. More like a rugged trail, that!" He reached down and picked out some of the briars and detritus he'd collected from the undergrowth, sighing at the mud splattered on his new Oxfords.

Yet here he was, finally at the wizard's small cabin. It looked just like the old witch in the tavern had described; wooden door, mud walls, and thatched roof. Fingering the protective charms in his pocket: the rune, shamrock, and rabbit's foot, he surveyed the clearing, looking for any obvious traps. He chuckled to himself.

"I've gotten myself a bit spooked, what?" He thought about the warnings the gnarled toothless woman had muttered. Rabid dogs. Firebolts. Swarms of man-eating insects. Yet all looked calm.

Nathan recalled the dozens of charlatans he'd had to suffer in search of his mother's ghost. There'd been so many disappointments that he had almost given up his hunt. But this one, this fellow might be different.

He thought back on how he'd finally found him. By digging through yellowed manuscripts and listening to whispers in dark chambers, he'd followed vague clues to the witch. From her, he'd found the wizard, the one reputed to have supernatural powers.

The wooden door creaked open. There stood the wizard, looking surprisingly modern with open wide collared shirt and a big cigar in his hand. His wild silver hair, mischievous smile, and round glasses made him look eccentric. He was old, though how old was difficult to say.

The soothsayer took one step into the yard and looked around. Catching sight of Nathan, he beckoned. "Come on in, young fellow. I've been expecting you."

With another squeeze of his rabbit's foot, Nathan fixed on a cocky smile and sauntered across the clearing into the wizard's hut.

Placing a hand on his chest to quiet his heart's flutter, he looked around in amazement. The inside of the hut appeared three times as large as the exterior. It had shining metallic walls decorated with small blinking lights. All sorts of machines sat in shelves or tumbled in various heaps on worktables. Many of them were clocks, perhaps a hundred of them. Some had hands like Nathan was used to. Others actually had numbers shining bright red.

The wizard took a seat in a stuffed green armchair and indicated for Nathan to sit in a similar red one across from a coffee table. On top of the table sat a spinning device that constantly changed colors and shapes. Nathan had a hard time taking his gaze off of it.

"You like the whirligig, eh?"

Nathan blinked, looked up at the wizard, and indicated the room with a sweep of his hand. "Name's Nathan. Nice place you have here."

The wizard put his head back and laughed. "Oh yes, nice place. I can just imagine what a roaring twenties hipster must think. Well, don't worry about it, Nathan Greenwell. Nothing here will hurt you."

Nathan raised an eyebrow. "How do you know my name?"

"Oh, I know all about you – who you are, what you want, and what's going to happen to you. My name's Mortimer, or at least, it will be for you. I'm also known as the Time Traveler."

"You travel through time?"

"Oh yes. And you will too. Here, before we start, let's have some refreshments." Mortimer grabbed a small black box that had been resting on the table and pressed a button on it. The whirligig sank into the table, and in its place glasses of ice water, a plate of grapes, and a long-stemmed white pipe surfaced.

Nathan grabbed the water and downed it. "Not as easy as a jaunt down High Street, getting to your place, what?"

"Not like your London alleyways, true enough. Have some grapes."

Nathan ate one, finding it uniquely tangy. "Delectable, old chap. Hit the spot, precisely." Nathan finished them off and then sat back. "What next?"

"Time is precious," Mortimer said, "so let's get down to business. You've been searching for information about your mother, Nathan. What do you remember of her and your father's home?"

The young man shook his head. "Teeny-weeny. Thirty-eight years ago? I was only two when she blinked out and Pater sent me a scurry. Of the old mansion, I recall a few snatches of images: a rug pattern, a set of huge wooden doors, some old portraits."

"We can work on your memory." Mortimer picked up the pipe, placed its stem to his lips, lit the bowl, and took a long inhalation. He released the smoke in little floating rings that drifted into nothingness. He passed the pipe across the table.

Nathan copied his host, finding the smoke had a gentle taste, much milder than a jag. A few seconds later he felt a fuzziness appearing around the objects in the room. When he spoke, his words tumbled out like a notebook bouncing down a staircase, pages flying everywhere.

"Why I'm here ... my mother ... must remember."

Mortimer sat forward speaking softly. "Think back, Nathan. Remember being a child of two. What was it like?"

Nathan's mind raced with images and voices from his past. "Frosh joyful days. We resided in a royal mansion, built by grandpapa. Carved wood, marble fireplace, a huge downstairs. My pater was an icy fob then, mader … can't remember. Lonely life, no playmates."

"What objects did you play with?"

"Objects? Hmm."

An image called for his attention. Only a snippet, the scene lasting but a few seconds. He described it for Mortimer. "Some old servant and self, settled on the Chinese rug in the salon. We were rolling a ball back and forth."

"The ball! Concentrate on the ball. What was it like?"

"The ball? Hmm. Metal, hard, and cold. Slots circumed the sides. A bob at top."

"That's the Silver Globe, Nathan. Remember it. Now sip the coffee. It will clear your head."

Nathan looked down at the table, finding that it now held only a steaming cup of coffee. He drank some and felt his head clear.

"Do you remember the Silver Globe, Nathan?"

"Precisely, and I'm just as certain I have no suggestions as to where it's tarried off. I imagine Pater tossed the old thing in the rubbish years ago."

The wizard clucked three times. "No, it's waiting on you in your bedroom closet. It's the key to your adventure as it will bring you to your mother."

Nathan stared at the wizard, and then shifted his gaze around the room. So many machines! Clearly this old fellow had magical powers.

"So, you're saying I need to go back to the Greenwell Mansion and retrieve the globe?"

"Yes. And you'll need this book." The wizard handed him a thick bound tome.

Nathan placed it on the table and opened it to its middle. At the top of each of the facing pages sat a strange symbol. Below each, notes had been written in various languages and obviously by multiple different hands. He recognized one in German, another in French.

"And what am I to do with this?"

Mortimer chucked. "You've always liked puzzles, right?"

Nathan shut the book and took another sip of the coffee. "You pander in impossibilities, old brainchild. If said silver ball resides on said bedroom shelf, it's verboten for my returning to Greenwell, on penalty of losing my inheritance."

A saddened expression came over Mortimer's face. "Ah, I'm afraid that's the other news I have for you, Nathan Greenwell. Your father passed away last night. His lawyer will be sending you a cable, possibly already waiting for you at your hotel. The inheritance is yours."

Nathan felt coldness sink into his heart. His father dead? The man who had financed his life, his only living relative, now no more? Nathan squeezed his eyes shut, trying to hold back the tears. "Are you certain?"

Mortimer nodded. "It's all part of your story. That's why I waited until today to allow you to find me. Now you'll head back to Greenwell Mansion and learn how to use the Silver Globe."

"My pater … he said I should never come home."

"No, he said you should never be seen in Greenwell. There's a subtle difference. Of course, you don't have to go back. You can have the bank send you money, let the local solicitors handle your affairs, and live the rest of your life in Europe. It would make you happier."

Nathan bit down on his lip. "No. I must tend to obligations."

"Of course you must." Mortimer stood and indicated for Nathan to do so. "You have a good two-hour hike back to your hotel. It'll be dark in three, so you'd better get going."

Nathan picked up the book and held out his hand.

Mortimer took it in both of his. "One more bit of information. The Silver Globe only works once per user. Now, have a safe journey, my boy."

Chapter 8

2017

"Have you finished figuring it out?" Allie asked, looking over Marley's shoulder as he fiddled with the silver sphere.

He set the ball back down beside the notebook and the pile of tiles. "Yeah, I've got it now." He picked up the instruction book, thumbing through the pages. "Nathan made notes on each page as he translated the foreign instructions. Each tile represents a time span. This purple one with the triple swirls on it stands for thirty-thousand days, which is eighty-two years and seventy days. We want to go back to March 12 of 1890, which is 127 years and forty-two days. That comes out to 46,427 days, remembering that 1900 was not a leap year and 2000 was."

He rummaged through the tiles, sorting them by colors and designs. "Once you know how many days you want to go back, you have to find the right combination of tiles, and know which slots to put them in. You have to have the metronome running at exactly one second intervals to orient the inner workings of the sphere. And, on top of all that, you have to align the compass on the sphere's point to magnetic due north."

"Why do you suppose Nathan wants us to join him there and then?" Allie asked.

"He said the date is exactly one week before his birthdate. Something to do with meeting his mother, no doubt."

"How do we get back to the present?"

Marley turned to the last page. "According to Nathan's notes, we turn the sphere to the south, remove the tiles, and we'll reappear in the space where we left, and at the time we left plus the time we were gone."

He replaced the book and the tile he'd picked up to the tabletop. Indicating a small stack of tiles he'd set to one side, he said, "According to my calculations, these are the ones we'll need for us to leave tomorrow at noon."

Allie gave him a kiss on the forehead. "Good. I'm almost ready. I'm just making my last-minute choices on which of the period outfits to bring. I have to remember we're visiting an isolated home that has totally different cultural mores. Not knowing how long we'll stay is another issue. And hardest of all has been your requirement that we can't bring anything that couldn't be made in 1890. You know how many things have plastic in them?"

Marley followed his wife out of the study and into their bedroom where she had clothes strewn out across their bed. She'd separated them in piles: underwear, skirts, blouses, shoes, and other accessories.

"Wow!" Marley said. "That's quite a collection. What's this thing?"

"It's called a bustle. A woman placed it over her rump to make her rear-end more prominent, and also to help keep the dress from dragging on the ground. Look at all these folds and pleats! There's at least twenty pounds in each of these dresses. And this blouse with the laces across the front? It's called a bodice. No jeans and t-shirts for these ladies!"

"Stockings too?"

"According to my research most women of the time wore black stockings, but that was in the big cities. In little Greenwell they still might be using 1870 fashion, which was white silk with little patterns like this." She picked up one pair and ran it across Marley's arm. "Soft, right?"

Marley stroked her cheek. "Fashion choices aren't so hard for me." He picked up a jacket, smoothing it out against his chest. "Narrow lapels, tight across the chest, and a collar close enough to nearly choke. I'm wearing this one tomorrow. Otherwise, I've got my suitcase packed." He pointed to the period bag sitting beside his dresser. "The shaving equipment required dangerous looking straight blades, but at least we won't have to smuggle them past TSA."

They both laughed.

"I'm glad your father was able to get us period money," he said. "The bills were quite pricey and harder to pass, so he concentrated on silver dollars, dimes, nickels, and Indian head pennies, about two hundred dollars in that box all total. Apparently, a little bit of money went far in those days. You could buy a gallon of milk or a pound of flour for fourteen cents."

Allie sorted through her clothing, choosing which items would be most useful. She picked up a box she had placed on the corner of the bed and opened it, revealing a small collection of jewelry and makeup.

"I've put together some gifts that should please the women. And no need to ask, I've made sure there's no plastic or other items inappropriate for the time. Well, most of the makeup are modern chemicals, but that shouldn't be a problem, as they'll be used up or decayed within a year."

Marley rubbed his chin. "Those sound like fine gifts, but will they make a long term difference? What if you could bring something that would help the plantation prosper, but wouldn't be out of time?"

Allie cocked her head. "What do you have in mind?"

"Well, I'm bringing bug-resistant high-yield strains of wheat, cotton, and corn. Although they're modern strains, no one there will see them as anything more than seeds."

"Hmm. Okay, I'll think about it."

The next morning, they had Sidney and Louise drive them to the town square with all their gear. They unloaded it beside the middle where fresh grass had been laid out after Daniel's statue had been removed.

"How do you know this is a safe spot to travel from?" Louise asked.

"According to my research," Marley answered, "the town square was open grass except for a gazebo in the middle of the park. In1893 or so the gazebo was replaced with the statue honoring Daniel Greenwell. And, of course, this is the spot that Nathan told us to launch from."

The Ames helped them arrange their bags and tied them together and to the Robbins.

"Are you sure this will bring your baggage with you?" Sidney asked.

Marley shrugged. "No idea. We're sort of flying on the wing here."

"We can't experiment with test jumps," Allie explained, "because the Silver Globe only works once per person."

Marley set the metronome on top of one of his suitcases and set it clicking. He had already placed the appropriate tiles in the designated slots on the sphere. Lifting it up he and Allie both placed their hands on it, the compass pointed down.

"Countdown to noon," he called out to Sidney.

Using his watch, the old historian called out the numbers each second, counting down from ten. When he got to one, Marley twisted the ball so that its compass faced due north. A dizzy feeling came over the couple as they popped out of twenty-first century existence.

Chapter 9

1930-1943

Nathan anticipated that Greenwell Mansion would be in a mess. From the letters he'd received over the prior few years, it was clear that his father, eighty-five when he died, had slipped into dementia. The weirdness began with mentions of his being cursed. Over the last two years, Daniel was rambling on about the ghosts of his brother Bobby and an old servant roaming the home at night.

Much to the solicitor's consternation, Nathan refused to meet directly with him, using George, the only house servant, as intermediary. Daniel's portfolio had involved a wide spectrum of assets, such as bank notes, land deals, loans to local businessmen, and railroad stocks. It took Nathan two years to straighten everything out.

He found plenty of money in the mansion. Federal currency, treasury bonds, and stacks of silver sat secure in the family safe. He discovered jewelry and gold coins stashed in various places; hidden drawers and cabinets seemed to have been a specialty of his grandfather during the house construction.

The house had been neglected near desperation. Replacing the roof, wiring, and plumbing had all gone smoothly. He enjoyed his new bathroom, complete with modern toilet, shower, and French style bidet.

Yet, except for new wiring to prevent fire hazards, he'd left the other bedrooms untouched. Each room spoke of its prior occupants. George slept in Daniel's boyhood room, keeping it clean and neat. The armoire there still held Daniel's old uniform, and a shelf held a few souvenirs from Daniel's youth.

His uncle Bobby's old bedroom had been locked, and Nathan had to get a locksmith to replace the hardware. Every time he stepped inside; Nathan felt chills. Bobby's Union uniform wasn't in his closet, though some of his Union insignia were.

The master bedroom could have been taken right out of the 1890s. The twin dressers each held gender specific clothes; on the top of one, men's haberdashery items, and on the other, half used containers of make-up and perfume. Nathan realized his father must have kept his mother's area just as it had been for the past thirty-eight-years, since the day she'd died.

The small office could fit little more than a lamp and a rolltop desk with its chair. The desk held papers and ledgers, stacked on top and stuffed into cubby holes. The desk drawers were so filled they could hardly be opened. As he leafed through them, his attention was grabbed by a detailed drawing of a doll. Although the paper was dated 1888, the doll looked exactly like a Raggedy Ann, a brand that hadn't been created for another thirty years.

His own bedroom held only a crib and a small dresser. He ordered all new furniture, including a radio and a telephone. He'd found the Silver Globe sitting on a shelf in the closet just as Mortimer had promised. Next to it, a bag held a selection of multi-colored tiles with foreign symbols. He moved these to the shelf above his bed.

He had brought a Ouija board back from Europe, as well as a crystal reputably useful for communicating with the dead. After the first year, he decided to try having séances. For his first attempt, he set up his crystal, the board, and gathered some of the items from his mother's dresser; a blouse, a perfume bottle, and a hairbrush. In the grand room he placed a table in a pentagram with candles and dark lighting.

"Spirit of my mother, send me a message," he chanted.

The planchette on the Ouija board didn't move.

"Spirit of my mother, show me a sign," he called again.

A chill came to the room, causing Nathan to shiver. The candles flickered.

Nathan was uncertain what to do next. This might be the spirit of his mother trying to communicate, or maybe some other spirit. Perhaps his mother had been illiterate, so wouldn't be able to spell out anything. Over the next few weeks he tried again three times, but a candle flicker was the most he got.

He decided to try other family members. With Thomas and Daniel, the responses again were minimal. Then he decided to try his uncle Bobby. He expected no response, based on his prior attempts. His belief that Bobby had run off in 1866 would indicate minimal ties to the property. Nevertheless, he figured to give it a try. He gathered a few of Bobby's personal items and set up his séance.

"Bobby Greenwell, send me a sign."

Nathan startled as the Ouija board's planchette began to move.

"Is that you, Bobby?" he asked.

The token crept across the board, settling on the "Yes."

"Do you have a message for me?"

The candles flickered and then flared. A glow developed near the fireplace and coalesced into a human-like figure, a ghostly shadow. Nathan stood; his mouth open in astonishment.

The ghost sailed from the fireplace towards the staircase, floated upward, and disappeared.

After that experience, Nathan left his Ouija board on his shelf.

Every evening since his arrival he'd devoted at least an hour to deciphering the book Mortimer had given him. He discovered that each page related to one of the tiles, and below each tile drawing, different people had made notes about what they had decided the tiles meant. Many were in scripts he couldn't read, Arabic, Russian, Greek, Chinese, and Hebrew, and he ordered translation books from around the world.

In all it took Nathan twelve years to translate all the information in the book. He learned about the ball's compass and the use of the metronome. He deduced that each tile represented a number of days or parts of days. He figured out that by placing the tiles in appropriate slots in the ball, he could go back in time by an exact time interval. Because there wasn't any displacement in the other three dimensions, only in time, he'd have to launch from a place that he knew would be safely empty at his destination time.

He chose to go back and find his mother a week before he was born. He figured it would be easy to determine who was his mother by searching for the most pregnant woman in the area.

As for the place, he considered materializing somewhere on the plantation, but decided it might be too disconcerting to those living there. He decided that he'd prefer to show up in town and act as if he were a visitor from Britain. His strange accent would certainly make him out to be a foreigner, and he could dress the part.

From studying his father's papers, he found that the statue to his father had been started the year after he was born, and until then the town green had held a gazebo. The statue was still there and using that as a take-off point seemed like a safe spot.

He rummaged for appropriate period clothing from a cedar trunk, kept bug free by moth balls. From it he chose a high neck frock coat with white collar band, an elegant tall top hat, and underlying vest. He found a period suitcase in the attic, and put together a week's worth of clothing, including toiletry items.

He slipped out of the house at eleven at night, carrying his bag and the Silver Globe, the proper tiles in their slots. Walking down the hill and through the town, he encountered no pedestrians, only a single car passed him. He mused that the depression hadn't hit rural Alabama as much as most of the country … they had started out with hardly anything to lose. Now, with the war taking many young men to Europe and the rationing of petrol, the streets of small towns in Alabama had little night traffic.

It was just before midnight when he arrived at the town square. Using a flashlight, he checked the globe tiles one more time, waited until his watch reached exactly twelve, and then flipped up the Globe to align its compass to North.

He felt dizzy and had to kneel to the ground with his eyes closed. He heard songbirds and felt the sun warm his skin.

Opening his eyes, he found himself next to the gazebo on the town square, just as he had planned. The only other people in the square were two white folks, a couple dressed in over-fancy clothes for the time, surrounded by several suitcases.

They startled at seeing him, and then came up to him, the man reaching out his hand to help him up. Nathan realized immediately they had to be foreigners. No locals would help up a black man. He was even more startled when the man spoke to him.

"Nathan Greenwell! A pleasure to meet you in the flesh."

Chapter 10

March 12, 1890

Nathan shook the stranger's hand and acknowledged the woman with a nod. "You have me at a disadvantage, sir."

Marley patted him on the shoulder. "Well, we haven't actually met in person before," Marley said, "but you told us to meet you here." He pointed to the Silver Globe Allie was holding. "See? We used your book and globe to figure out how to get here."

Nathan stepped over and Allie handed him her globe. Comparing the two, he couldn't see any difference, except for which tiles were in the slots. "The Time Traveler didn't tell me there was more than one Silver Globe."

"There's not," Marley said. "This is the same one, but in a different time loop I would say."

"Time traveler?" Allie asked. "Who is that?"

"It'd take too long to explain," Nathan said. Turning back to Marley, he asked, "I'm a bit confused. You say we've never met, but I told you how to use the machine and to meet me here? How is that possible?"

Marley smiled and shrugged. "It'd take too long to explain." They all laughed.

Nathan looked around the green. In the thirteen years he'd been back to Greenwell, he'd snuck into town about a handful of times, all but once at night. Forty years had brought a lot of changes. The town looked different in many ways; dirt roads instead of pavement, horse-and-buggy instead of automobiles, gas lights instead of electric. Several of the buildings were different, although a few of the stores from his time were here now.

The biggest differences were the people. Women shopped with their servants carrying their parcels. White men lounged in big chairs while blacks polished their shoes. A young black boy hawked a newspaper next to a fruit stand offering peaches.

"There's a wump of difference from 1943," Nathan said. Turning to Marley, he asked, "From what year did you originate?"

"2017. Except for the courthouse, none of these buildings still exists."

Nathan whistled. "Wow! I bet you have amazing widgets in your time. Did you tromp in with moderns to show?"

Marley and Allie both shook their heads. "No anachronisms if we could help it," Allie said. "But we did bring gifts."

"We're eager to know what we're doing here," Marley said. "You told us where and when to come, but you didn't tell us why."

Nathan took his handkerchief and wiped his brow while he composed his thoughts. "Ever since I was a tot of nine, I've been on a quest to root out my mater's heritage," Nathan explained. "She died when I was quite young, and my pater refused to tell me anything about her. Gawd, I don't even know her name. Do you?"

"No, we haven't found any information about her," Allie answered.

Nathan raised an eyebrow. "Well, I bloody well must have had motivation in recruiting you to join the force; so, please give me your skinnies."

"We're the current owners of the Greenwell Mansion in 2017," Allie explained. "We've been interested in your family history since even before we bought it."

"So now that we know when, where, and why, tell us the how," Marley requested.

Nathan looked from one to the other. "My scheme runs blatant. Present at said homestead and gander for the lady with the belly swelling."

Allie grimaced. "Do you really think that's a good plan?"

"Why not?"

"We're in 1890, you're an African-American, and this is Daniel Greenwell you're talking about."

"African-American?" Nathan laughed. "Is that the nomenclature for Negros in your days?"

He scratched his chin as he observed the town's pedestrians. Growing up in Europe, he had known little discrimination. Secluded in his home, his perspective on how blacks were treated came mostly from George's viewpoint, which limited his understanding. Even so, here social structure seemed more rigid, with a deference paid by the blacks, assumed by the whites, that seemed demeaning. And threatening.

Turning to his new friends, he asked, "What do you suggest?"

"I have an idea," Marley said. "What if we say Allie and I are visitors from somewhere, Raleigh for example. We'll say you're our manservant. That way you can be accepted in the home and have a chance to make inquiries."

"Hmm, I like it," Nathan said.

"We can be reporters for one of their papers," Allie suggested. "The Raleigh Register had a wide circulation in those days. We can be writing an article about how the South has recovered from the War for Southern Independence."

"Brilliant, as ever," Marley said, giving her a kiss on the forehead.

Turning back to Nathan, he said, "The first thing to do is hire a coach."

Nathan bit his lip. "Hire a coach? I confess to lack of funds."

"We have money." Marley pointed to a carriage shop across the street. "You two wait here while I go hire us a ride." He strode across the street.

Allie sat down on a park bench, but when Nathan started to join her, she shook her finger at him. "You've got to learn to act the part, Nathan."

"Yes, ma'am," he said with a nod, standing erect next to her. "So, Allie, how is the house doing?"

"Everything's hunky-dory since we got rid of the ghosts and found the treasure under the body. Oh! Maybe I wasn't supposed to tell you any of that. I don't want to mess up history."

Nathan cocked his head. "Hunky-dory is a term I'd use. I'm surprised it still exists in your day. Ghosts? Treasure? Dead body? Perhaps it's better if you don't spill the beans."

"Instead," Allie suggested, "tell me about your life. You never kept a diary, at least, not that we've found."

Nathan gave her a summary, telling how he'd been to boarding school and prep schools until age 18, followed by four years at the Sorbonne. For the next eighteen years, with plenty of money and time, he'd been traveling, exploring Europe. These enjoyable years of exploration, searching for secrets into talking with the dead, came to an abrupt end when his father died. He returned to Greenwell and snuck into the house where he'd been secluding for thirteen years.

"Since my return," he continued, "I've been repairing the homestead, minding the store, and elucidating this zany time traveling ball." He stopped and pointed across the street. "It appears that Marley's flying the flag."

He offered Allie his hand and helped her stand up. "By the way, what am I to call you?"

"Master Marley and Miss Allie sounds appropriate."

With the help of the coachman and an assistant, all the luggage was loaded into the back of the carriage. Marley and Allie took the back seat and Nathan the driver's bench.

"I told them you'd handled horses before," Marley called up to him.

Nathan shook his head. "First time for everything." He clicked the reins and the horses trotted down the street. After a few minutes, he got the feel for how to guide them and the three enjoyed the pleasant mile and a half trot to the edge of town, up the hill, and onto the driveway of the Greenwell Mansion.

The carriage was met there by two men and a teenage boy, all dark skinned. One of the men and the boy were barefoot, wearing only overalls. That man took the reins from Nathan and handed them to the boy. The other man, dressed in black slacks, a white shirt, and polished shoes, reached out a hand to help Marley and Allie out of the carriage.

"Welcome to Greenwell Mansion," the servant said. "I be Hany, the butler."

Marley handed him an embossed card which read, "Marley Robbins, investigative reporter."

Hany stared blankly at the card and back at Marley.

Marley gave him a smile. "Please tell Mr. Greenwell that Marley and Allie Robbins from the Raleigh Register have come to call."

"Yes sir. You folks wait up 'ere on the porch and Mabel'll be bringin' y'all lemonade."

The Robbins settled onto rockers while Nathan stood attentively at their side. In a few minutes Mabel appeared, offering a round of lemonade to all three. Just as she finished, Hany stepped out again. "Master Daniel say he be righ' down." Having made his announcement, he left them alone.

As promised, the homeowner soon appeared, shook their hands, and settled into a third chair. "What brings you folks all the way from Raleigh to little ol' Greenwell?"

Marley gave him the story Allie had suggested about being reporters. "Greenwell has a well-earned reputation," he continued. "Besides the cotton sales, your brick factories and horse breeding are well known across the South, even up to Raleigh. It seems like all is thriving here."

"We're doing all right," Daniel admitted. "Had to cut back on cotton without the slaves to pick it. We're growing a new crop, soybeans they call it. And, as you say, the other businesses are doing well."

"Quite well, apparently," Marley said. "You've been very generous to the town, funding several buildings and improvement projects. I hear they're going to put up a statue to you on the town green."

Daniel stood and stared down at him. "How do you know that?"

Allie spoke up, "We heard rumors in town, that's all."

Daniel looked between the two of them. "That's very strange. No one is supposed to know anything about that yet. The mayor was here only two days ago proposing the idea."

He sat down again and laughed. "Small town – rumors spread quickly I suppose."

A very pregnant woman came out on the porch. "Hany said we have visitors?" She was quite beautiful, looking to be late teenage or early twenties, with smooth light skin, shining eyes, and perfect gleaming teeth. Except for her slightly broad nose, she could have passed for a pure Caucasian, a Russian beauty.

Marley stood and performed a slight bow. "Marley Robbins, and this is my wife Allie." He indicated Nathan, who had stepped forward from his position against the wall, now standing wide-eyed and slack jawed. "This is our man servant, Nathan."

Daniel, who also had stood on her entry, introduced her. "This is Ginger, the woman of the house. She's in charge of all the servants."

"It's a pleasure to meet you," she said. "Will you be staying for dinner?"

"We wouldn't want to impose," Allie said.

"Nonsense," Daniel replied. "You two can settle into the guest cabin. Ginger, have Hany arrange for it to have fresh bedding and linen." Turning back to the Robbins, he said, "Hany will find a suitable room for your servant as well."

"I could stand to freshen up," Allie said.

"Of course." Ginger took her hand and led her inside.

"Before dinner, we could take a tour of the plantation," Daniel suggested to Marley, who readily accepted the offer.

Nathan stood quietly, staring at the door where Ginger had disappeared.

Chapter 11

March 18, 1890

When she saw Allie approach, Ginger patted the spot next to her on the bench. Allie settled there, under the large willow by the creek. They held hands, eyes closed, listening to the frogs serenading in the evening air. A heaviness hung in the air, as if rain might fall soon.

"I'm so glad you came to visit," Ginger said. "I've been terribly lonely."

Allie gave her a kiss on the cheek. "Why are you lonely? You don't have friends among the house staff?"

Ginger shook her head, looking out across the fields where one-foot-high green corn stalks showed the beginnings of the spring crop. "It's not just that the servants are busy, it's more that … well, I'm different. I'm in a special social class, too upper for the blacks and too low for the whites. Do you understand?"

Allie patted her hand. "I guess so. Why doesn't Daniel ever have guests so that you can make friends?"

"He says he was traumatized by the war and feels more comfortable alone." She stared down at her hands in her lap. "I think it's because of me. I suspect he thinks the other white folks will look down on him if they knew he was consorting with a woman of mixed blood."

"He clearly loves you," Allie said.

Ginger closed her eyes and sat back, her pregnant belly like a watermelon on her lap. She rubbed it as she began sobbing.

Allie reached over with her handkerchief and wiped away the tears. "Do you want to talk about it?"

She shook her head, and then nodded. "He loves me, I know that. But he won't tell me so. I'm good enough to sleep with, good enough to have his baby, but not good enough to marry. I sometimes wish I'd never had anything to do with him. I thought if I had his baby, he might accept me fully, marry me. After all, I'm three quarters white, and look nearly all white, don't you think so?"

She turned to face Allie. "Don't you think so?" she asked again, pushing in her cheeks, squeezing her nose. "I bet if I went to a big city, Montgomery or Chattanooga, I could pass as white. I've worked on my language, can't you tell?"

Allie furrowed her brow. "Ginger, my dear. You don't need to be white. You're lovely the way you are."

Ginger snorted. "Not in Alabama, I'm not. I should have known better. I should have just found a fine black man to marry, like …." She stopped and looked down at her belly again.

"Like Nathan?"

Ginger looked up; her eyes wide. "What did he tell you?"

Allie held up her hands in defense. "He didn't have to tell me anything. I can see it in both of your eyes, the way you look at each other. This week together has clearly been an opportunity for you two to get to know each other."

"Oh, he's wonderful – everything I ever imagined a man could be! Brave, gentle, wise, sophisticated. He's seen so much of the world, traveled throughout Europe. If I weren't where I am, pregnant and entrenched here, I'd run off with him in a moment!"

"Have you told him that?"

Ginger pulled herself up and walked down the path away from the house. She stood at the creek bed, plucking out a bulrush and rubbing its soft bristles against her face. When Allie came up to stand next to her, she saw tears streaming down her cheeks.

"I did. I told him I loved him. He told me he loved me too, but that he had to go away. He says I'll be delivering the baby tomorrow morning and y'all will leave that evening. Oh, I mean, all of you." Ginger took hold of Allie's shoulders, looking into her eyes. "Is that true?"

Allie nodded. "I guess so. We've been here a week. We've probably already worn out our welcome."

Ginger squeezed her eyes shut, more tears dribbling out. "I'll always remember you. If I have a girl, I'll name her Allison."

"And if it's a boy?"

A half smile turned up on Ginger's cheeks. "Nathan, after the first man I truly loved."

Allie took off her wedding ring, placing it in Ginger's palm and closing the woman's hand around it. "This is for you."

Ginger examined it; eyes wide. "Oh, it's gorgeous! I can't possibly take this."

"This is going to sound strange," Allie said. "But someday you'll give it back."

Chapter 12

March 18, 1890

Marley pumped gently with his foot, enjoying the slight rocking of the chair as he sipped the whiskey Mabel had brought out to the porch. He smacked his lips. "This is good stuff!"

Daniel chuckled. "Yep. It's called Jack Daniels – made in Lynchburg, Tennessee. I have three bottles shipped down here every month. They say it's the water that makes it good, but I'd put my money on the aging. To get good whisky, you've got to age it in oak barrels."

They sat quietly for a bit, the setting sun below huge gray clouds turning the fields to a golden scarlet, and then fading to gray.

"We'll be leaving tomorrow evening," Marley said. "I can't tell you enough how much we've enjoyed your hospitality."

"It's been my pleasure. I'm very appreciative for the gifts you've brought: the disease resistant seeds, the reading glasses, and the fine leather belt. The gifts your wife brought for Ginger certainly cheered her up, those sweet-smelling perfumes, canisters of make-up, and the herbs for the garden. What'd you call them?"

"Basil and thyme."

"Yep, yep. Nice. As I say, we don't git many guests out here, except some of the city folks asking for donations. You're a might different from them. Raleigh News you say?"

"Yes."

"Not the Observer?"

Marley hesitated. "Uh. No, that's our competitor."

Daniel took another few sips of his whiskey. The night birds had started their calling, the deep moan of the mourning doves giving way to the barn owl's hoot.

"Now isn't that strange?" Daniel asked. "It's been ten years since the two newspapers merged."

Marley flushed. "Um. Well, we just call it the News now, I guess."

Daniel finished his drink, set it on the table, and took out two cigars. He offered one to Marley, who waved it off. After lighting his, Daniel took a few puffs before speaking again.

"Why don't you tell me the truth now, Mr. Robbins? It's clear you three are from somewhere else. You and your wife sound like you're from Alabama, but the words you use aren't quite right. And your clothes," he waved the cigar in Marley's direction, "look like you never learned how to put them on. It's got something to do with those metal balls you got there, right?"

Marley swallowed. "You're not going to believe me."

"Try me."

"Okay. We're from the future. Allie and I bought this house in 2015. We traveled back these hundred plus years to see what it was like in this age. We're looking to refurbish our home in period pieces."

Daniel finished off his drink and puffed a bit more on his cigar. He put it out in the tray and called for Mabel to bring him more whiskey. After she refilled both of their glasses, he sipped a bit more before breaking the silence.

"Strangely enough, I believe the part about you being from the future. However, there's something more y'all are after than decorating ideas. Why not just tell me?"

Marley took a deep breath. "Very well, sir. We'd like to know what really happened between you and your brother."

Daniel glanced his way and let out a rough laugh. "Police?"

"No, sir, not at all. But we did discover your brother's body behind the fireplace, and the gold. Also, Joseph's body with the knife and your fingerprints on it. As I said, we're from the future, so we're not looking to change anything. We're just curious. I mean, now that I've met you, you're much, well, nicer than I had predicted. I wouldn't peg you for a murderer."

In the distance a coyote howled, the call being picked up in a chorus by several of his cousins. The smell of jasmine and camellias drifted onto the porch with the evening air.

Marley thought of how different the world of 1890 was from 2017. No car sounds. No sirens. No gasoline smells. No electric lights disturbing the night sky. Above them the milky way shimmered in all its glory.

He pondered for a moment whether life was better in these days – no deadlines, no air pollution, and practically no crime. Yet the advantages of his time were immense; entertainment, transportation, cell phones, Internet, and, perhaps most important of all, health care. Life expectancy in 1890 was 48. People died of polio, smallpox, and dozens of other diseases that modern medicine had defeated. No, he preferred the safety of his own time instead of a nice view of the sky.

"Bobby always was a brat," Daniel recounted. "Mother favored him, spoiled him really, and he felt he deserved to be given everything. When the war came, he ran off to join the damn Yankees. Probably a good thing, actually. Made a man of him. He came back toughened, but meaner than ever."

He paused to take another sip of whiskey. A bat swooped past; its high-pitched screeches just barely audible.

"Bobby came back thinking he could run the Greenwell plantation better than me. He was making foolish decisions and contradicting my orders. He'd only been here a month when he found out about the gold. That's when things got bad. He announced that he deserved half of it."

Marley interrupted. "Tell me about the gold."

Daniel stood and walked over to lean against the banister, looking down at Marley. "I was assistant secretary of the treasury for the Confederacy under George Trenholm. You know anything about Trenholm? No? Well, he was a genius. South Carolina businessman and merchant. Built a fleet of schooners that ran the Union blockade and made a mint.

"During the last days of the Civil War, Trenholm had all the confederate bullion holed up in Richmond banks. As the Yankees closed in, he told me to move it onto a train headed for the new capitol in North Carolina. Well, I knew that was a fool's mission. Instead, I hid it in the false bottom of a carriage and managed to sneak it out at night, and all the way home. Now it's mine, and it's been financing the rebuilding of Greenwell Plantation and the city of Greenwell. It's Southern money going to a good Southern cause."

Marley rose and leaned on the rail as well, although several feet away. The night sky had delivered a chill. Clouds obscured the stars and the wind kicked up small whirlwinds.

"You were telling me Bobby was being difficult," Marley said. "What happened the night he died? I read that you told all the servants to leave you two alone."

Daniel grunted. "June third. That date mean anything to you?"

Marley shook his head.

"Really? Ever hear of Jefferson Davis?"

"Of course, president of the Confederacy."

"That's right. Died last year. I gave everyone three days off to celebrate his birthday. Only our butler Joseph stayed. He'd roasted a pig for Bobby and me for a private celebration. Yes, sir. Eating pork. Drinking whiskey. Having a grand old time."

Daniel paused, staring off across his land, no doubt seeing the ghosts of the many people who'd lived and died here. "And then … we weren't. He started going on and on about how the North had beaten the South down, and I called him a traitor, and the fight escalated."

A boom of thunder came from nearby, the lightning creating a flashing of white across Daniel's face, although he didn't flinch. In a minute a heavy rain pummeled the dirt, sizzling against the rocks heated by the day's sun. He spat over the railing; the foam washed away by the rain.

"Bobby grabbed a kitchen knife and hurled it at me. I saw it coming and stepped aside. Unfortunately, Joseph was standing behind me and the knife buried itself in his chest. He died instantly. Bobby had his sword with him, he always did, some type of manly issue, I think. He started chasing me around the kitchen with it. As I passed the knife rack, I grabbed the butcher knife, spun around and sliced off his hand at the wrist, the sword clattering to the floor. He fell stone backwards, smashing his head on a pan."

Daniel called out to Mabel who hurried out with the whiskey and refilled his glass. He downed it in one gulp and stood still, staring at the empty cup.

Turning to Marley, he demanded, "What do you think, Mr. Robbins? Does self-defense ever excuse someone from murdering his brother?"

Marley spread his hands. "I can't answer that."

"No, I suppose not." The rain stopped as quickly as it came. The moon peeked out from the dissipating clouds.

"I buried Joseph in with the family, he deserved that much." His chin jutting, he turned to stare down Marley. "Bobby didn't, so I entombed him behind the fireplace. I figured he wouldn't be found for a long time. Seems I was right."

Marley's mouth was so dry he couldn't speak. All this time he had presumed the worst of Daniel. He wet his lips. "Your fingerprints on the knife in Joseph's chest?"

Daniel snorted. "It was stuck so tight I couldn't get it out, so I just buried him with it embedded."

Marley stepped over and placed his hand on Daniel's shoulder. "Thank you for the explanation."

Daniel shrugged. "At night, sometimes, I seem to see their ghosts, Bobby and Joseph, walking the halls. I guess I'll always be haunted by them."

Chapter 13

March 19, 1890

Nathan sat on the cane chair next to Ginger's, who was rocking as she breastfed her ten-hour-old baby. He watched them, his heart pounding with the realization that this would be the last time he'd ever see his mother. She was so lovely, so gentle, so sweet, so … motherly. He had fallen deeply in love with her.

"The baby seems healthy."

Ginger smiled, her white teeth glistening in the evening sunlight. "Yes! I'm so happy. He'll grow into a strong man, a lot like you! He even looks like you."

Nathan winked. "He has my skin color." He noticed Ginger's smile disappear. "What?"

She took the baby off her breast and placed him against her shoulder, patting gently on his back until he burped. Cleaning off his spit with a towel, she moved him to the other breast where he latched on eagerly.

"You're right. Despite being only an eighth black, it seems that he'll have dark, dark skin. It's not fair."

"Oh, that can't be so bad."

She looked at Nathan with scorn. "You grew up in Europe, so you don't know. Here, dark means inferior. Here in Alabama he'll be scorned, offered only menial jobs. He'll grow up with head and back bowed, half a man."

Daniel came out on the porch and leaned against the rail. He struck a match against his shoe sole and brought it up to light the cigar he had clenched between his lips. In the distance gunshots echoed. A flock of geese took off in the air, honking loudly.

Ginger finished burping the baby again. Holding him out, she asked, "Do you want to hold your son?"

Daniel hesitated a moment before stepping over and picking him up. The two stared at each other and the baby smiled. Nathan saw Daniel's hardened face soften, the hint of a smile he'd only occasionally seen on his father's face on the thirty or so yearly visits he'd made to Europe to visit him.

Daniel handed the baby back to his mother. "You did good, Ginger. What're you going to name him?"

Ginger glanced at Nathan before turning to look Daniel in the eyes. "I want our boy to grow up to be a leader. He should be educated in the ways of the world. When old enough, we should send him to prep school in Europe. In other words, I'd like him to be just like our visitor here," she indicated Nathan, "and so I've named him after him. Did you know Nathan means 'Gift of God'?"

Daniel turned his gaze skyward, taking a series of puffs from his cigar and blowing them out. Turning to look at Nathan he cocked one eyebrow. "'Gift of God,' huh? Well, I like that name.

And, I must say, I'm impressed with our visitor. You're an unusual nigger, ain't you? What's your full name?"

Nathan grabbed a name from the news he'd been reading before making his trip. "Nathan … uh, Churchill, Mr. Greenwell. My father was a landowner."

Daniel fiddled with the cigar some more before grinding it out on the banister and throwing it into the bushes. "Yeah, you sound like a foreigner all right. I hear tell you and the Robbins are fixin' to be leaving tonight."

Nathan stood. "Yes sir. We're very grateful for your hospitality."

Daniel brought two more cigars out of his pocket and offered one to Nathan, who accepted it. Daniel lit them both and they puffed in silence for a minute.

"Going back to your own place and time, I gather. What is your place and time, anyway?"

Ginger looked back and forth between the men. "Whatever do you mean, my love?"

Daniel snorted. "He knows what I mean."

Nathan allowed his gaze to slowly scan the view from the porch, starting at the far corner and turning slowly past Daniel and Ginger to end up looking at the mansion's front door. He pointed at it casually with his thumb, and then at the baby in Ginger's arms.

"It's not a coincidence that Ginger picked that name, sir."

Daniel startled, staring first at Nathan, then at the baby, and then back at Nathan. "You mean …"

Nathan stepped forward and Daniel took him into his arms in a hug. Nathan whispered, "I love you, Pater."

Daniel stepped away, pulled a handkerchief to his eyes, turned abruptly, and strode into the house.

Ginger shook her head. "What just happened? I've never seen Daniel hug a man before."

Nathan smiled and shrugged. "It's a brace for bruno."

For another five minutes they stood, watching each other. Nathan spoke, "I'm on a drift, have to dust out. We're fading in just a bit." He stepped over and reached out his hands. "May I hold the baby once more?"

She handed him over and Nathan cuddled him, tickling his nose and cooing. "Ah, sweet young man. Although you try to be lammed, you'll never escape the Greenwell legacy." He handed the baby back.

From under her chair, Ginger picked up the Raggedy Ann doll, hugging it to her chest, and then holding it out for Nathan.

"This doll is the first personal possession I ever owned. It was given to me by the old woman who midwifed me at my birth. I've always loved it, pretending it was the baby I would have some day. Well, now I have a real baby, and I'd like you to have my doll as a reminder of me, Nathan. Will you treasure it?"

Nathan took it and held it tightly against his chest. "Yes," he said softly through his tears. "I'll treasure it always."

Chapter 14

2017

The four friends sat around the mansion's dining table, enjoying the savory pork roast Allie had prepared. Gershwin's "Rhapsody in Blue" played softly in the background as the sweet smells of roasted potato with garlic tickled their noses. The familiar furniture and artwork of the refurbished mansion brought comfort as Marley and Allie told their tale.

"That's truly amazing," Sidney Ames said. "You experienced history as it happened. I know I've asked you a thousand questions, and I'm sure I'll ask you a thousand more. Like, tell me how the geese looked when the gunshot went off? Were there a thousand of them, in a cloud so thick you could barely see the sky?"

Marley laughed. "No, not that many. I've read that was true when the first colonists came in the sixteenth century, but by the end of the nineteenth, geese had already been reduced to small bands."

He finished off his wine, refilling his glass and those of the other three.

"Oh, how I'd love to see it for myself," Sidney said with a sigh. "To actually experience history, to witness how people lived … hell, not just witness, but actually be part of it. It's every historian's dream."

Marley glanced at Allie who smiled and nodded. Turning back to Sidney, Marley said, "You're about to have the opportunity to fulfill that dream."

"What do you mean?" Louise asked.

Marley pointed to the Silver Globe and bag of tiles sitting at the far end of the table. "You know that Nathan told us the time traveler said the Globe will work only once per person. Since Allie and I have had our turn, we'd like to give the ball to you."

Sidney gasped. "Really! Oh, yes! That would be fabulous. I'd love to go back to the 1850s, to really experience what life was like." He turned to Louise. "Would you like to come with me, my dear?"

Louise laughed. "Of course, my cherished one. Where you go, I go. How long would you like to stay?"

"Oh, a few months at least. Maybe a year or two. Would you be willing?"

Before she could answer, Marley cleared his throat. "There might be a complication."

Sidney raised an eyebrow. "What?"

"I've been thinking about how this all worked out. The Silver Globe exists only within certain time loops. Listen. Somehow, it existed in this mansion in the 1890s. When we were there three of the Globes existed: the one Allie and I had, the one Nathan brought from 1943, and one that already existed. The one Nathan had, he brought back to his present, and it sat on his shelf for many years. We picked it up and then used in our travels. Currently it sits on the table."

"I didn't follow all that," Louise said.

"The point is," Marley explained, "that somehow the Silver Globe was already in the mansion when we arrived with our two copies. Therefore, this Globe has to go back in time and stay there for Nathan to use and then leave for us."

Sidney let out a whoosh. "Oh, dear!" He looked from Marley to Allie, who nodded, and then he reached over and grabbed Louise's hands. "I would gladly do it. After all, I'm over seventy years old. But I couldn't ask such a thing of my lovely young wife."

Louise shook her head. "I still don't get it."

Allie got up and walked over to Louise, urging her to stand up in a hug.

"It's got to be a one-way trip," Allie explained. "Whoever takes the Globe to the past will give it to the Greenwells and won't have a way to come back."

Sidney stood and walked over to the globe, running his hands along its surface. "Of course, it's got to be me. At my age it's unlikely I'll live more than a year or two in an era with such poor hygiene and nutrition. Still, it will be well worth it to see what life is really like."

He looked over to his wife, still standing and holding Allie's hands. "You'll stay here, my love. You're only forty-five. You have many good years ahead."

Louise walked down the room and hugged her husband. "They wouldn't be good years without you. As I just said, where you go, I go, or, in this case, when. This will be a great opportunity to save lives. I can see myself being a midwife in those days, teaching others proper hygiene. You know, techniques were so crude in those days that infant and maternal mortality were huge. Just a little bit of instruction would save hundreds of lives.

They stared lovingly into each other's eyes.

The End

About the Author:

Philip Levin has published over thirty books and 200 articles, stories, and poems, many award-winning. His multi-genre output includes a murder mystery, ghost story, contemporary romance, historical fiction, Mississippi history and biographies, medical stories, poetry, children's books, and memoirs. Please find other books of his on Amazon or purchase from his website at www.Doctors-Dreams.com.

Recently retired from 42 years as an Emergency Medicine physician, he spends his hours pursuing a Masters in Fine Arts in Creative Writing, traveling with his French Girlfriend, and rubbing the belly of his lovable Pekinese Fluffy.

www.ingramcontent.com/pod-product-compliance
Lightning Source LLC
Chambersburg PA
CBHW070523130626
46555CB00003B/1321